Dedicated to my nieces and nephews:
Charles, Stacy, Matthew,
Ryan, Rick, Roger,
Ellie and John.

This book belongs to

For information address Toy Truck Publishing, 4602 Lilac Lane, Lake Elmo, Minnesota 55042

www.toytruckpublishing.com

Composed in the United States of America

Display text is set in CK Hopscotch

Edited and Designed by Joe Holmberg
Publisher Shelly Holmberg

FIRST EDITION

Library of Congress Cataloging-in-Publication Data

Stephas, Kristi.
Flying solo / by Kristi Stephas ; illustrator, Rachel
Smith.
p. cm.
SUMMARY: Six-year-old Ellie is flying alone for the
first time, taking an airplane from Chicago to see her
aunt in San Diego.
Audience: Ages 3-12.
LCCN 2004195574
ISBN 0-9764983-2-4

1. Air travel--Juvenile fiction. [1. Air travel--
Fiction. 2. Travel--Fiction.] I. Smith, Rachael.
II. Title.

PZ7.S8293Fly 2005 [E]
QBI05-800159

Flying Solo

Ellie is 6 years old and flying solo for the first time. She is flying all by herself from Chicago to San Diego to visit her Aunt Jen.

Author Kristi Stephas Illustrator Rachael Smith

Toy Truck Publishing
www.toytruckpublishing.com

“Ellie, are you going to take all night to pack your suitcase?” Ellie's younger brother, John, asked.

“Hold your horses,” said Ellie. “I'm looking for my swimsuit.”

"Here's your swimsuit," called Mom as she and Dad entered Ellie's bedroom. They helped Ellie finish packing and double checked to make sure she didn't forget anything.

"Well, Ellie, you're all packed," Mom said.

"And just in time for bed," said Dad. "John, say good night to your sister and Scruffy, and skedaddle back to your room for bed."

"Night night! Sweet dreams and don't let the bedbugs bite," giggled John as he ran out of the room.

Mom and Dad tucked Ellie into bed, turned off the light, and left Ellie in her familiar, sleepy darkness.

Ellie closed her eyes and imagined playing on the beach at Aunt Jen's house.

She pictured sandcastles, seashells, and the bright sun in the big, blue sky. And if she closed her eyes real tight, she could feel the sand between her toes and hear the waves crashing along the shore. Soon, she drifted off to a deep, deep sleep.

The next morning, the very sleepy-eyed Ellie was awakened by Scruffy, who had jumped on top of Ellie and was licking her face until she sat straight up in bed.

"Oh Scruffy!" she shouted with joy. "I'm flying to San Diego today!"

Ellie leaped out of bed, got dressed, and ran downstairs for breakfast.

John was already sitting at the kitchen table eating his favorite breakfast, a stack of blueberry pancakes smothered in syrup. He took a drink of juice and looked up at Ellie and asked, "Are you afraid to fly all by yourself?"

Suddenly Ellie got butterflies in her stomach. She hadn't thought about flying all by herself. All of her thoughts were about playing on the beach with her Aunt Jen and how much fun it was going to be.

Ellie turned to her Dad and asked, "Is flying solo scary?"

"Oh no, sweetheart. You know your mother and I fly all of the time. It's very safe. And there might be other kids flying solo. The flight attendants and pilots will take good care of you."

After breakfast, Ellie kissed Mom, John and Scruffy good-bye. Dad was taking her to the airport. He put her suitcase in the trunk so that when they arrived at the airport, unloading would be as easy as 1-2-3.

CHICAGO
123456

When they were close to the airport, there were a lot of cars. Some drivers were in a hurry. They honked their horns. Other cars just sat along the curbside and waited. Big jets and little jets were taking off and landing. It was a noisy place.

After they parked the car and walked inside the airport, Ellie's Dad said, “It's our lucky day. It's just a short line. This is where we check your suitcase and get your boarding pass.”

As they approached the ticket counter, Ellie's Dad handed the agent her ticket.

“Are you traveling to San Diego all by yourself?” asked the ticket agent.

“Yes, I'm 6 years old and flying solo!” Ellie said with a great, big smile.

“You're going to have a great flight,” responded the ticket agent. “Now that you've checked your luggage and you have your boarding pass, you need to walk through security and proceed to gate B-9; or as the pilots would say, Bravo Niner, Roger.”

At security Ellie and her Dad practically had to get undressed again. When Ellie realized she had to take off her belt and shoes, she wondered why she couldn't have just worn her slippers and PJs! She placed her backpack and the rest of her belongings on the conveyor belt and walked through the metal detector. Once they walked through the detector without beeping, Ellie's Dad gathered her belongings and together they walked to B-9.

"There's my plane!" shouted Ellie as they approached the gate area. And there it was indeed - a shiny, new 737 blue and red jet.

There were a lot of people waiting to go to San Diego. The gate agent announced that it was time to board the plane.

"Don't worry, Dad. Flying solo isn't so scary," she said and kissed him good-bye.

The gate agent walked Ellie down the jet way to board the plane. The flight attendant greeted her with a smile and said, “Welcome aboard! Follow me to the flight deck to meet the pilots and then we will find your seat.”

“This is Captain Artie and First Officer Ava, otherwise known as Ava the Aviator,” said the flight attendant. “They are both excellent pilots. They are going to make sure that you have a very safe flight to San Diego.”

The flight deck was very small with just two seats and a lot of buttons and knobs. Captain Artie invited Ellie to sit in the captain's seat. He showed her how they taxi to the runway using their feet to steer the plane. And when it's time for take off, they push the throttle all the way forward and pull up on the yoke.

The flight attendant told Ellie it was time to find a seat.

"May I sit next to the window?" asked Ellie.

"Of course," replied the flight attendant. "I will sit you next to the window along with two other children who are flying solo.

"This is Olivia, she is 8 years old. She flies with us once a month. Her parents are divorced. Half the time she lives in Chicago with her father and rest of the time she lives in San Diego with her mother. Olivia is a frequent flier. She has probably earned enough miles to fly around the world three times!

"And this is Charlie. He's 10 years old and this is his second time flying solo. He is traveling to San Diego for surf camp. He's a rad surfer!"

"All right now," said the flight attendant. "Everyone stow their backpacks underneath the seat and buckle up and we will be on our way!" Click - click - click. Three safety belts were clicked into place and they were ready for a smooth flight.

Ellie watched out the window. The ramp agents were loading the luggage into the belly of the plane. Once all of the bags were loaded and all of the passengers found a seat, a tiny tug pushed them away from the gate. As the plane taxied out to the runway, the flight attendants instructed the passengers on what to do in the event of an emergency. Their job is to make sure everyone on the plane has a safe and comfortable flight.

Captain Artie announced, “Flight attendants take your seats. We've been cleared for takeoff.”

The plane began rolling down the runway faster and faster. The ground was slipping away. Soon they were soaring in the air.

“Just sit back and relax,” said Olivia. “Flying is fun! Look out your window and watch the big city get smaller and smaller.”

Ellie looked out the window. She could see her neighborhood. The higher they flew the smaller the city became. The tall skyscrapers looked like marshmallows. The people looked like tiny ants and the cars looked like John's toy cars.

As the plane climbed higher and higher, a layer of clouds appeared and covered the entire city.

Charlie said, "Look at the clouds! They look like giant cotton balls! That cloud over there looks like me surfing a gigantic wave."

Olivia looked into the clouds and pictured herself flying to Paris with her frequent flier tickets.

And Ellie imagined John and Scruffy playing ball in the clouds.

FLYING SOLO MDW-SAN
FLYING SOLO MDW-SAN

"My ears feel funny," said Ellie as she tugged on her earlobes.

"Your ears just need to pop," said Charlie. "Chew this gum, it will help."

"Yawning makes your ears pop, too," added Olivia.

Ellie's ears finally popped and she felt much better.

Up in the air, the flight attendants passed out peanuts and drinks. After the service, Ellie's new friends kept busy reading and playing games. Ellie continued to look out the window. She couldn't take her eyes off the view.

The ride got a little bumpy. The flight attendant came by and told them not to worry about the bumps. They were flying over the Rocky Mountains, and those big mountains like to rock the passengers. Ellie laid her head against the window and looked down on the enormous snow-capped mountains.

Once they flew over the mountains it was back to smooth flying. The view was magnificent.

FLYING
SOLO
MDW-
SAN
PEANUTS
FLYING
SOLO
MDW-
PEANUTS

A few hours passed, and finally Captain Artie announced that they were approaching San Diego.

They heard the landing gear drop. Ellie looked down over the great, big, blue ocean. It was filled with sail boats, Navy ships, cruise ships and tiny tugs. The skyscrapers were standing tall along the ocean. The ants grew into people, and the toy cars were big again.

The three children flying solo were grinning from ear to ear. Ellie was excited to see her Aunt Jen, Charlie couldn't wait to go surfing, and Olivia missed her mom.

The wheels touched down and the plane came to a slow taxi. It was a great flight. Ellie felt proud of herself for being brave and flying solo.

They safely arrived at the gate. The flight attendant escorted Ellie, Charlie, and Olivia off the plane to meet their loved ones. Ellie's Aunt Jen was waiting behind a big welcome sign and a bunch of balloons. Charlie's surf counselor was there to greet him, and Olivia's Mom was waiting for her.

Aunt Jen hugged and kissed Ellie, then asked, “How was the flight?”

“It was great!” shouted Ellie. Ellie liked everything about flying. She liked the take off and landing. She liked looking out the window. But most of all, she liked meeting the flight crew and making new friends.

CHICAG

Ellie waved good-bye to Olivia and Charlie, then walked with Aunt Jen to baggage claim and picked up her suitcase.

"Now that you have your luggage, let's go to the beach!" exclaimed Aunt Jen.

"That's a great idea!" replied Ellie.

Ellie had a blast at the beach with Aunt Jen building sandcastles and finding sea shells. She loved the hot sun on her skin.

After awhile they took a break, and Ellie lay down on her beach towel and closed her eyes. She could feel the sand beneath her toes and she listened to the waves crashing along the shore. Soon she drifted off to a deep, deep, sleep.

She could hardly wait to fly solo again.

Tips for Parents When Kids Fly Alone

1. **Arrive early**: This alleviates anxiety and ensures the child a chance to preboard.

2. **Make a new friend**: Ask the agent if there are other children flying solo. If so, introduce the children to each other.

3. **Pack a healthy lunch**: Make your child's favorite lunch and include a treat or two. Avoid packing too much candy since they are required to remain seated for most of the flight.

4. **Pack a sweatshirt or a light jacket** in their carry-on. Planes are often chilly.

5. **Pack a favorite game or toy.** Hand-held electronic games may be used during flight.

To learn more, go to

www.toytruckpublishing.com

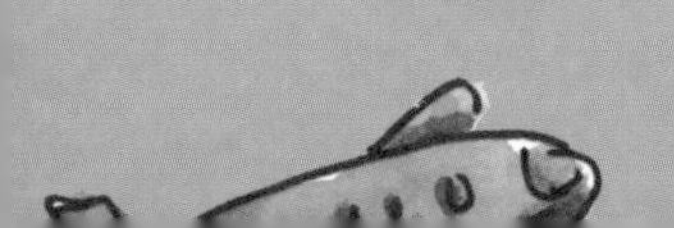
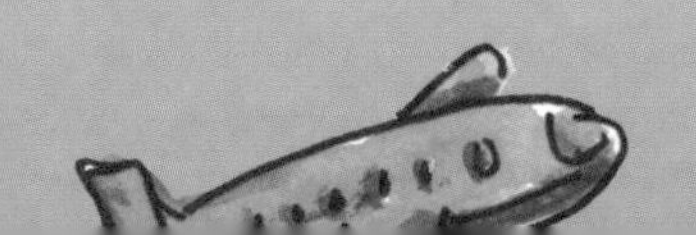